S0-AKB-250

DISNEY · PIXAR
INSIDE OUT

DISGUST

by **Brittany Candau**
illustrated by **Jerrod Maruyama**

DISNEP PRESS
Los Angeles · New York

I'm
Disg

ust.

You should know there are a *lot* of **gross** things out there.

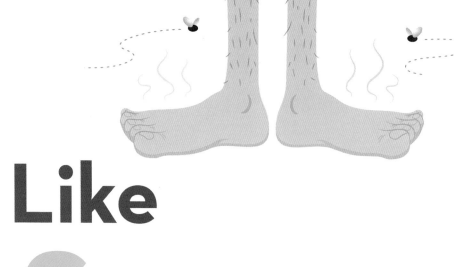

Like
feet.

Who decided people should walk around on

smelly blobs with toes sticking out the end?

Even the things that cover feet are gross.

PEEE-EWWWWWWW!

While we're at it—

crabs.

What are they even doing crawling sideways like that?

Or

I've got a disgusting word for you: *udders*.

Wanna know a lame activity?

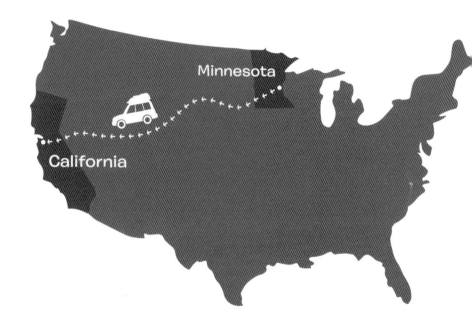

Going on a twenty-eight-hour road trip. In a tiny car.

Let me tell you, *nothing* is worse than hearing the same sad song sung off-key ... over and over again ... by Dad ... while you're trapped in the car.

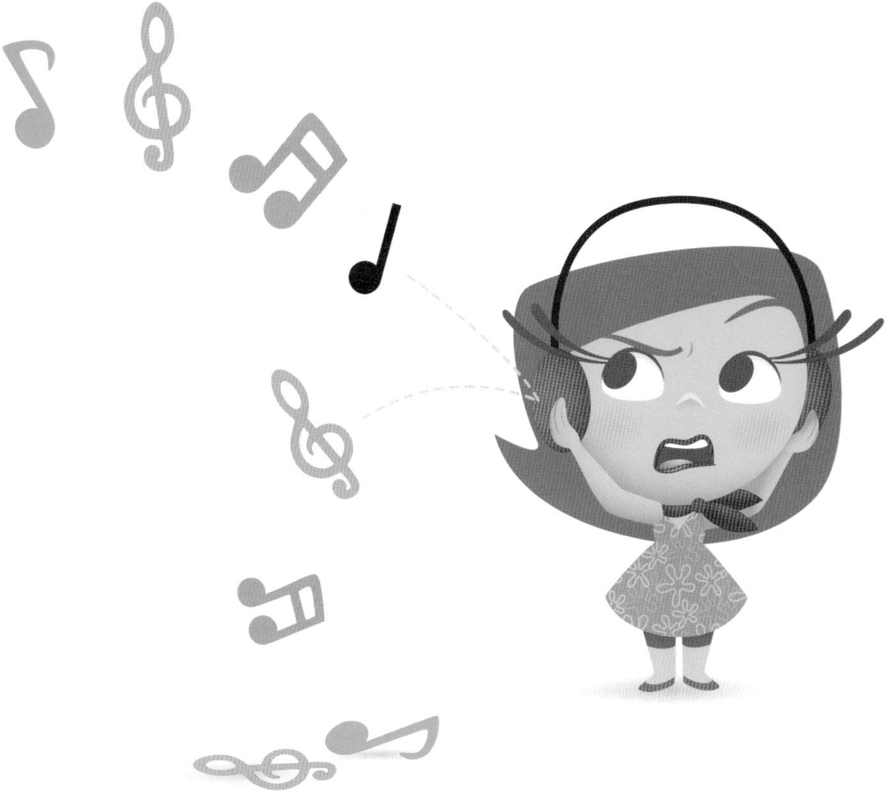

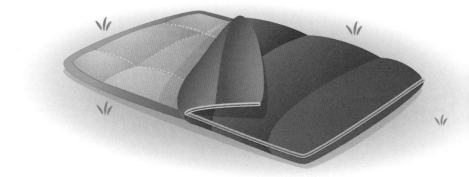

Except maybe sleeping on the

dirty
ground

Or sweating!

Ew.

Totally gross.

Or not

having any

running

water.

I don't do

smelly.

Or a dangling

spider.

And you know where all of these awful things happen? Camping. In the woods. Where there are all sorts of hairy wild animals and strange little bugs that can hop on you at any moment.

No,
thanks.

I'm done.